SALARIYA

© The Salariya Book Company Ltd MMXI

3 5 7 9 8 6 4 2

Visit our website at **www.book-house.co.uk**
or go to **www.salariya.com** for **free**
electronic versions of:
**You Wouldn't Want to be an Egyptian
Mummy!**
**You Wouldn't Want to be a Roman
Gladiator!**
You Wouldn't Want to be a Polar Explorer!
**You Wouldn't Want to Sail on a 19th-
Century Whaling Ship!**

A CIP catalogue record for this book is
available from the British Library.

Printed and bound in China.
Printed on paper from
sustainable sources.

Published in Great Britain in MMXI
by
Book House, an imprint of
The Salariya Book Company Ltd
25 Marlborough Place,
Brighton BN1 1UB
www.salariya.com
www.book-house.co.uk

ISBN-13: 978-1-907184-79-6

PAPER FROM
SUSTAINABLE
FORESTS

PROF. Zacharias Zog's

Splat-a-Fact

BATTLES
DOODLES
DOT-TO-DOT
PUZZLES!
MAZES
ART
DAFT STUFF
DOODLES
STUFF
SPOT THE DIFFERENCE
GAGA STUFF

Mummy
Activity Book

by
Prof. Zacharias Zog

and

Prof. Your name

Hiero-glyphs

joke!

A B C D
E F G H
I J K L
M N O P
R S T
X Y Z U

Walk like an egyptian

Splat-a-fact

HIEROGLYPHS, THE EGYPTIAN FORM OF WRITING, WAS CARVED ON TEMPLES AND TOMBS. FOR EVERYDAY WRITING A MORE JOINED-UP FORM WAS USED.

Write like an egyptian

K _ _ _ _ _ _ _ _ _ _ U _

CAN YOU WORK OUT WHAT THE HIEROGLYPHS SAY?

A: The Dead Sea!

4

Splat-a-Fact

'MASTABA' COMES FROM THE ARABIC WORD FOR 'BENCH'. IT'S OFTEN A SHAFT OR AN UNDERGROUND BURIAL CHAMBER.

MASTABA TOMB

HORUS

Can the God Horus find the Mastaba Tomb?

A FUNERAL PROCESSION

Magic Bricks

N

THE SYMBOL ON THIS BRICK
LIVED IN ANCIENT EGYPT

W —————————— **E**

THE SYMBOL ON THIS BRICK
REPRESENTS STABILITY

THE SYMBOL ON THIS BRICK
WAS A GOD.

THIS BRICK COULD BE LIT

S

A SET OF FOUR BRICKS
MADE OF MUD, FEATURING
DIVINE IMAGES OR SYMBOLS
OF GODS, WERE PLACED IN
THE TOMB. THESE BRICKS
HAD MAGICAL PROPERTIES.

HUMAN FIGURE

DJED AMULET

TORCH

CLAY ANUBIS FIGURE

Match the magic bricks

USING THE CLUES, MATCH THE
MAGIC BRICKS TO THE SIDE OF THE
TOMB THEY WERE PLACED.

CANOPIC JARS HELD THE BODY'S ORGANS. THE TOPS OF THE CANOPIC JARS REPRESENTED THE FOUR SONS OF THE GOD HORUS: IMSETY, DUAMUTEF, HAPI AND QEBEHSENUEF.

Canopic Jars

SPLAT-A-CLUE

HUMAN = LIVER

JACKAL = STOMACH

FALCON = INTESTINES

BABOON = LUNGS

MATCH THE ORGANS TO THE JARS

LIVER

LUNGS

INTESTINES

STOMACH

9

Bound for the tomb

MUMMIES GET THEIR NAME FROM THE ARABIC WORD 'MUMMIYA' MEANING 'BITUMEN', BECAUSE THE RESIN FOUND ON MUMMIES LOOKS LIKE BITUMEN.

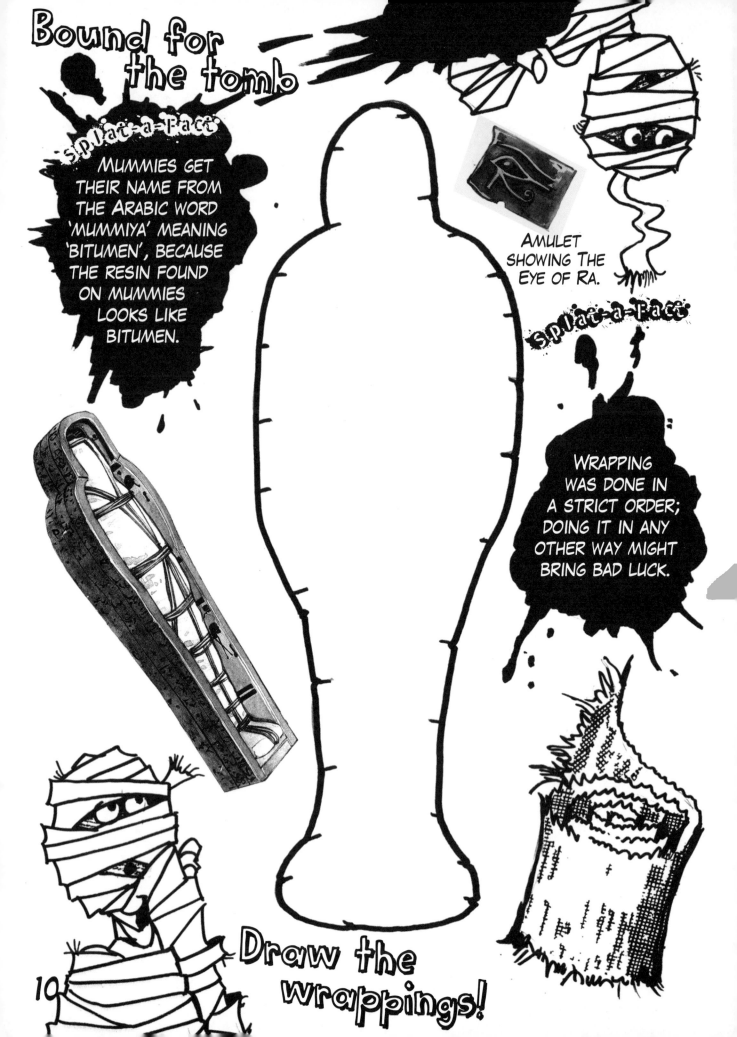

AMULET SHOWING THE EYE OF RA.

splat-a-fact

WRAPPING WAS DONE IN A STRICT ORDER; DOING IT IN ANY OTHER WAY MIGHT BRING BAD LUCK.

10

Draw the wrappings!

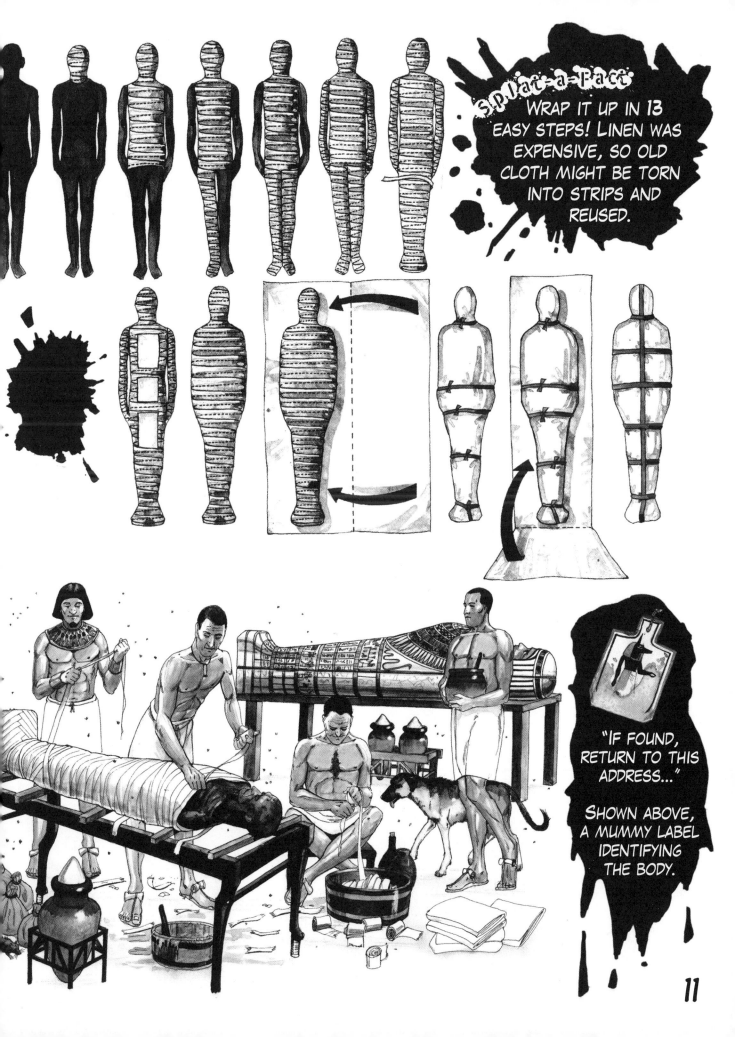

Splat-a-Face
WRAP IT UP IN 13 EASY STEPS! LINEN WAS EXPENSIVE, SO OLD CLOTH MIGHT BE TORN INTO STRIPS AND REUSED.

"IF FOUND, RETURN TO THIS ADDRESS..."

SHOWN ABOVE, A MUMMY LABEL IDENTIFYING THE BODY.

Splat-a-Face

TO JUDGE FROM HER PORTRAIT BUST, AKHENATEN'S CHIEF WIFE, QUEEN NEFERTITI, WAS VERY BEAUTIFUL.

AFTER THE COFFIN HAD BEEN CARVED IT WAS PAINTED WITH GESSO, A MIXTURE OF CHALK AND GLUE. THEN THE CRAFTSMAN PRESSED ON THIN SHEETS OF GOLD.

Splat-a-Face

Draw Queen Nefertiti's face and headdress

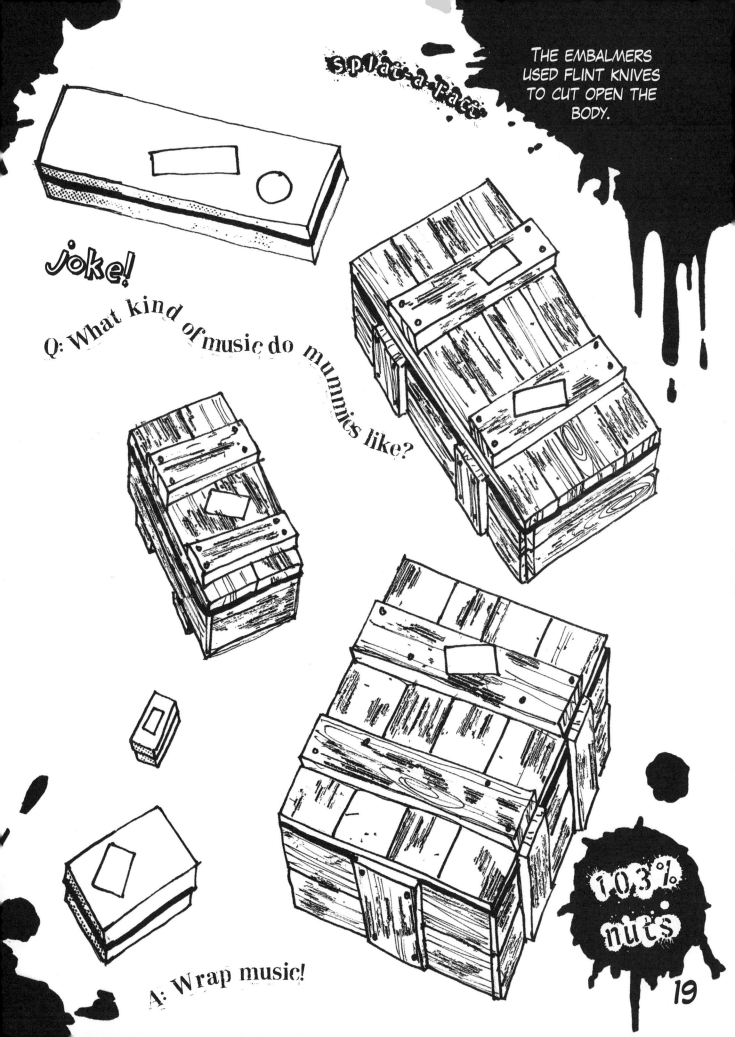

splat-a-fact

THE EMBALMERS USED FLINT KNIVES TO CUT OPEN THE BODY.

joke!

Q: What kind of music do mummies like?

A: Wrap music!

103% nut's

19

First, break the seal

Finish decorating the walls of the tomb with paintings.

IN THIS ROOM, DRAW THINGS THAT THE PHARAOH WILL NEED

Q: What did King Tut say when he got scared?

joke!

A: I want my mummy!

DRAW WHAT'S IN THE SECRET CHAMBER

How many scarab beetles can you find?

Add some treasure!

Colour in the tomb

Draw yourself as a Pharaoh or Egyptian princess

Use a mirror to help you

Joke!

Q: What do you say to an annoying scarab?

What are the Egyptians saying?

Make up an Egyptian joke!

THE OPENING OF THE MOUTH CEREMONY REAWAKENED THE MUMMY'S SENSES SO HE OR SHE COULD 'LIVE' IN THE NEXT WORLD.

24

Wrapping it up!

A carpenter's tool box would have contained:

A plumb-line weight

An adze

A round-bladed axe

An awl

Two chisels

A bow drill

A PRIEST DRESSED AS THE JACKAL-HEADED GOD ANUBIS SUPERVISED THE WRAPPING OF THE BODY, AS IN THE PICTURE ON THE LEFT.

AS WELL AS HUMAN BODIES, EMBALMERS MUMMIFIED THE BODIES OF ANIMALS, SUCH AS CATS AND BABOONS WHICH WERE SACRED TO THE EGYPTIANS.

Can you join the dots to make a mummy mask?

splat-a-fact

THE BODY WAS COVERED IN NATRON (A TYPE OF NATURAL SALT) AND LEFT TO DRY OUT FOR 40 DAYS.

Draw around your own hand to create a death mask
on the opposite page

joke!

Q: How did brave Egyptians write?

A: In hero-glyphics!

THE HEART WAS LEFT IN THE BODY SO IT COULD BE JUDGED GOOD OR BAD IN THE NEXT WORLD.

Splat-a-Fact

COLOUR IN THE MASK AND ADD DETAIL

29

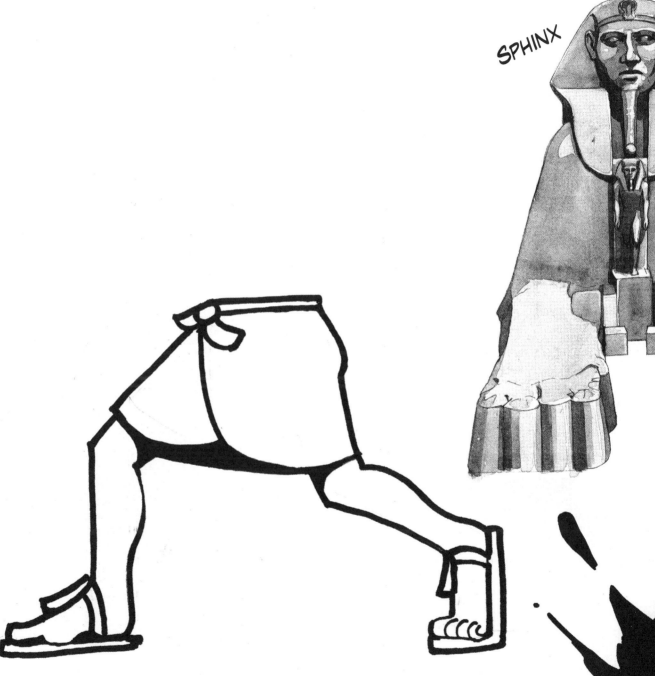

SPHINX

Walk like an Egyptian...

How to draw a really scary mummy

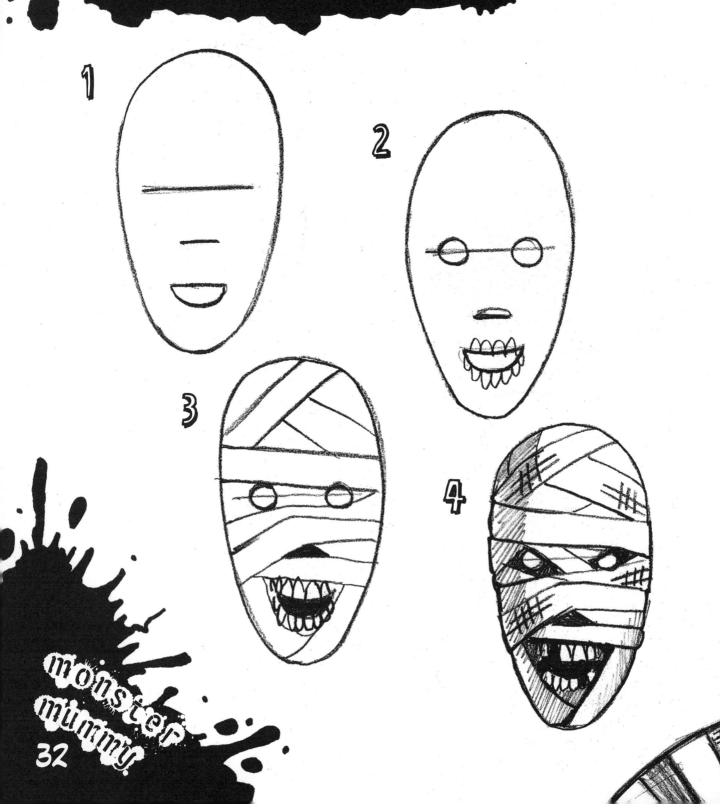

joke!

Q: How did the doctor know that the mummy was ill?

DRAW YOUR
OWN MUMMY
HERE

A: He was coffin a lot!

GGRRR

33

What's the mummy?

All wrapped up

Give each mummy a funny name

MUMM-O-SAUR?

37

Colour in the crowns

THE NEMES CROWN HAD A COBRA AND VULTURE'S HEAD TO REPRESENT THE KING'S PROTECTORS.

THE QUEEN'S HEADDRESS FEATURES NEKHBET, THE VULTURE GODDESS OF UPPER EGYPT.

joke!

Q: What kind of sweets do Egyptians eat?

38

How many mummy cases can you find on these pages?

NOW, YOU HAVE A GO!

47

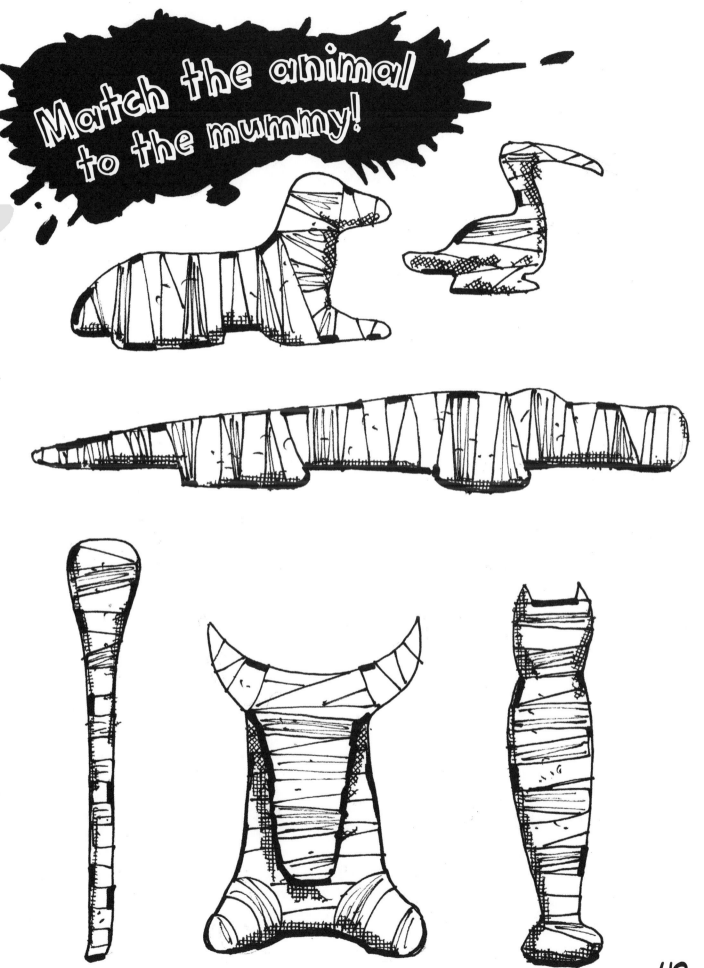

How many mummies can you find in the town?

Splat-a-fact

THE EMBALMER WOULD SHOW YOUR FAMILY WOODEN MODELS OF VARIOUS STYLES OF MUMMY: CHEAP; MID-RANGE AND LUXURY.

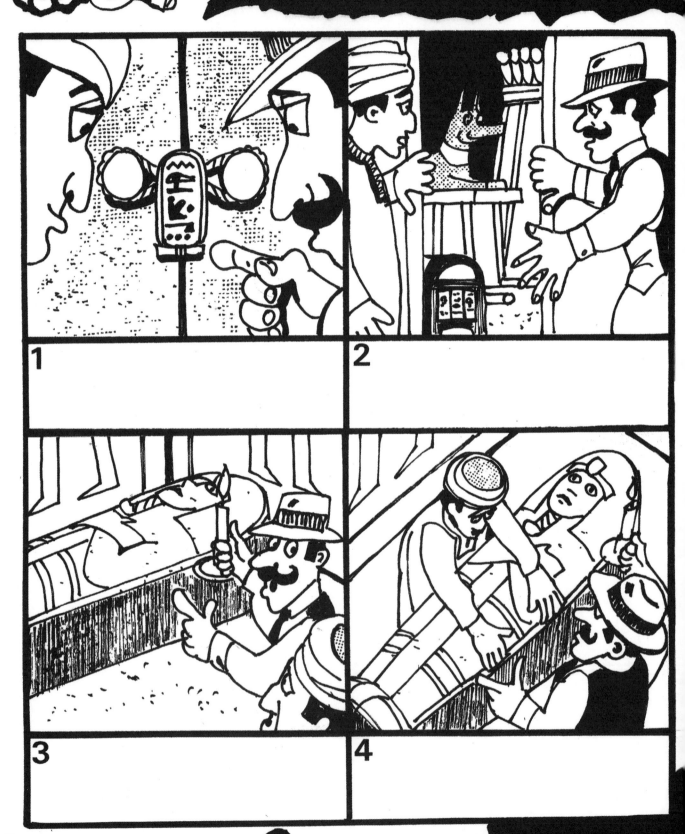

1

2

3

4

THE VALLEY OF THE KINGS WAS REDISCOVERED BY HOWARD CARTER WORKING FOR THE WEALTHY ENGLISHMAN LORD CARNARVON.

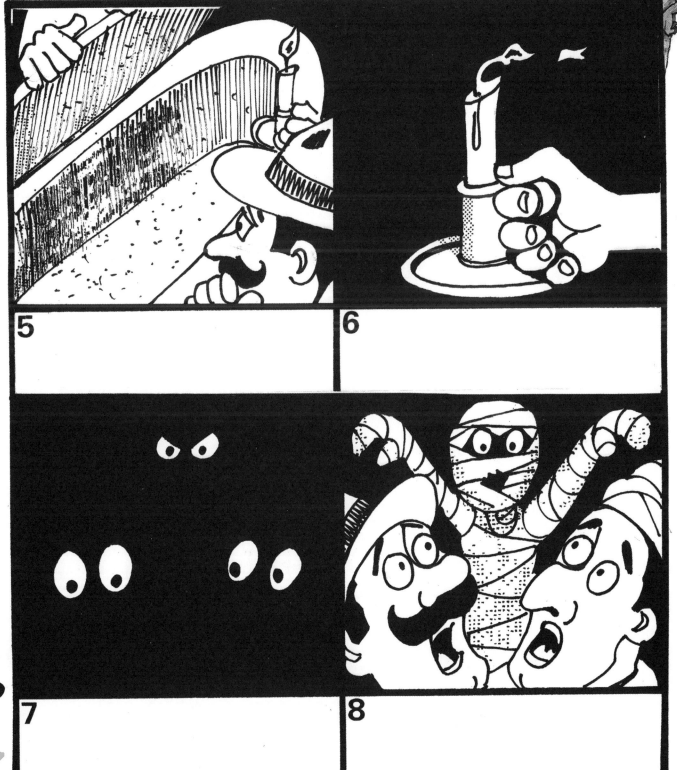

Mummy Wordsearch 1

CHEST

JAR

M	F	J	Q	E	D	B	P
U	N	C	H	E	S	T	K
M	S	L	V	J	P	O	N
M	P	Y	R	A	M	I	D
Y	Y	K	M	R	F	R	R
B	E	U	K	F	S	T	A
C	Z	Y	O	W	X	A	I
Y	S	C	A	R	A	B	J

SCARAB

MUMMY

PYRAMID

COFFIN

USE THE CLUES TO FIT THE WORDS INTO THE CROSSWORD

WHERE A MUMMY IS BURIED

T _ _ _

A WRAPPED UP BODY

_ _ M _ _ _

LUCKY CHARM

A _ _ _ _ _ _

_ Y _ _ _ _ _ D

TRIANGULAR BUILDING

EGYPTIAN KING

P _ _ _ _ _ _ H

EGYPTIAN PAPER

_ _ P Y _ _ _ S

55

How to draw a manic mummy

1

2

3

joke!

Q: What did the mummy say when he heard a silly joke?

splat-a-draw

58

Find the sarcophagus

A-maze-ing!

1

2

3

4

SADLY, MANY MUMMIES WERE DESTROYED WHILE BEING UNWRAPPED FOR 'ENTERTAINMENT'.

Splat-a-patt

QEBEHSENUEF

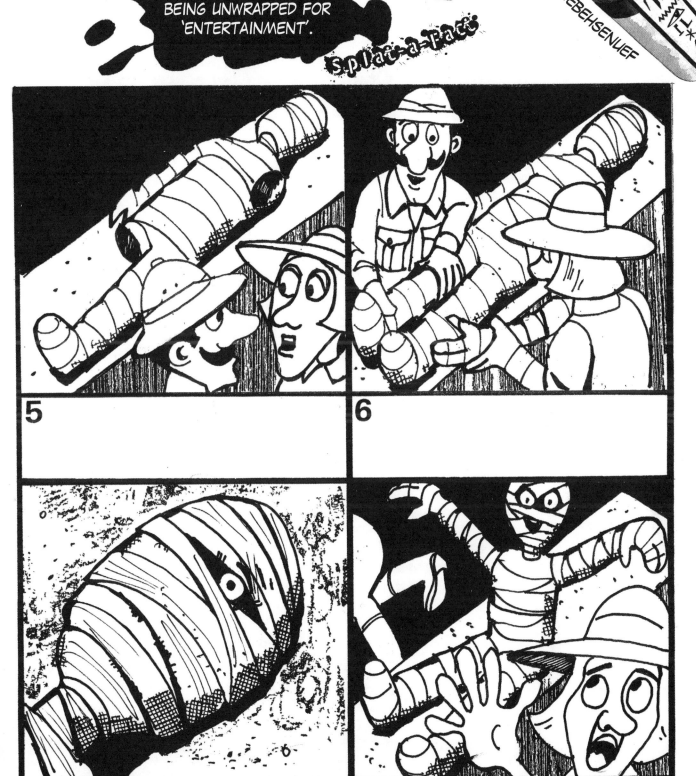

5

6

7

8

Draw the mummy
from the previous
page from memory

HOW'S YOUR
MUMMY
MEMORY?

How to draw a Sarcophagus

1

2

3

splat-a-draw

joke!

Q: Why don't mummies go on holiday?

4

A: They're afraid they will relax and unwind!

DRAW YOUR OWN HERE

FINISH THE DRAWING OF THE SUN GOD RA!

70

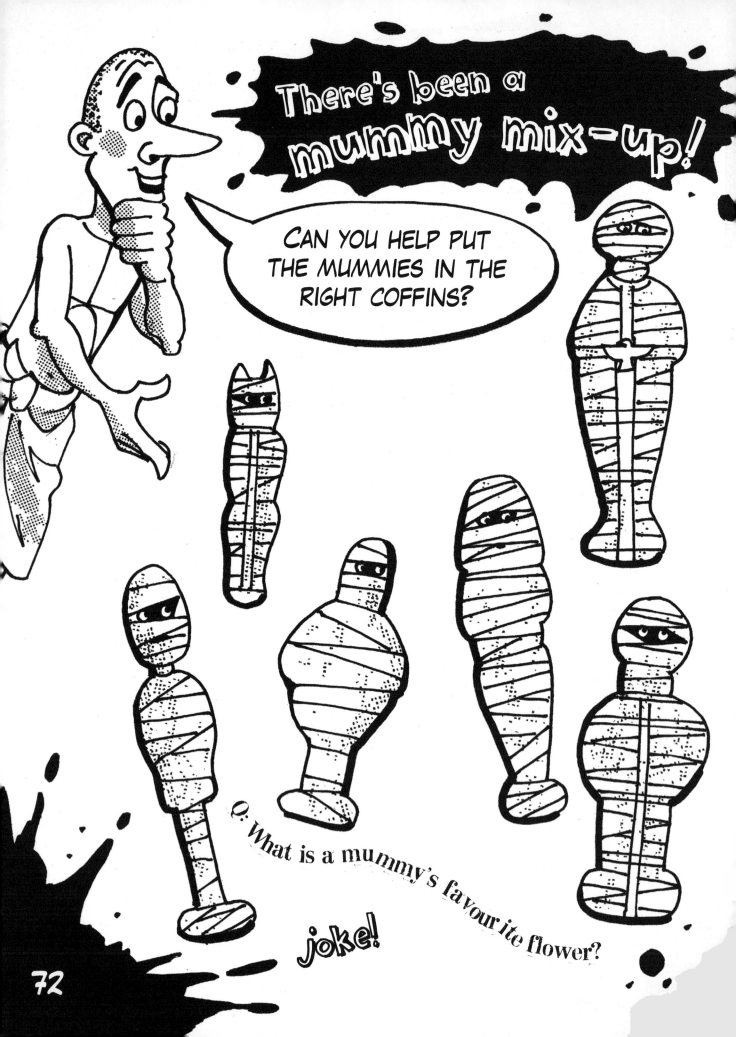

A: Chrysanthemummies!

Seth

GOD OF CHAOS,
CONFUSION AND
VIOLENT WATER

WHO WILL
WIN?

SPLAT-A-BATTLE

Horus
PROTECTOR OF
EVERY PHARAOH

WRITE BELOW
THE GODS THEIR
SPECIAL POWERS,
FIGHTING SKILLS
AND STRENGTHS!

FIGHT!

Splat-a-Fact

BOATS PLAYED SUCH AN IMPORTANT PART IN THE LIVES OF THE EGYPTIANS THAT THEY WERE SOMETIMES PUT IN TOMBS.

EXIT

Help me!

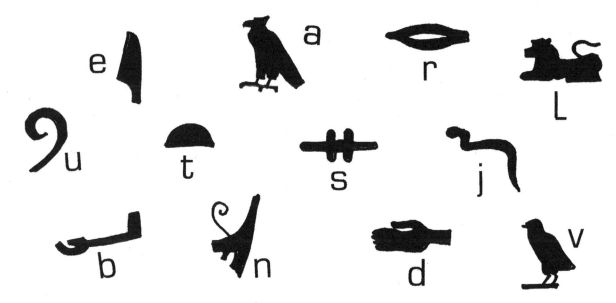

LEGEND HAS IT THAT GEORGE WASHINGTON (1732-99), FIRST PRESIDENT OF THE UNITED STATES, WORE FALSE TEETH MADE OF WOOD. ACTUALLY, THEY WERE MADE FROM HUMAN AND ANIMAL TEETH. HUMAN TEETH WERE OFTEN OBTAINED FROM CORPSES, OR FROM THE MOUTHS OF THE VERY POOR, WHO SOLD THEM.

WHERE'S MY TOMB ENTRANCE? BREAK THE CODE TO FIND OUT.

PUT ME BACK TOGETHER!

splat-a-fact

IN JANUARY 2005, EGYPTIAN RESEARCHERS CARRIED OUT A CT SCAN THAT PRODUCED 1,700 IMAGES OF TUTANKHAMUN'S MUMMY. THEY FOUND THAT HIS LEFT THIGHBONE HAD BEEN FRACTURED AND BECAME SEVERELY INFECTED JUST BEFORE HIS DEATH.

Mummy crossword 2

MUMMY

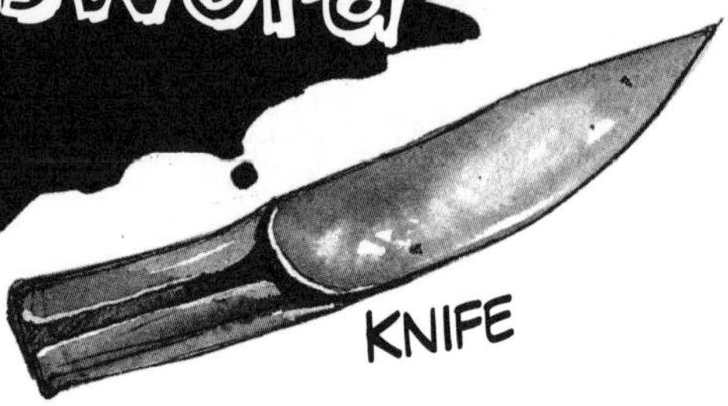

KNIFE

AXE

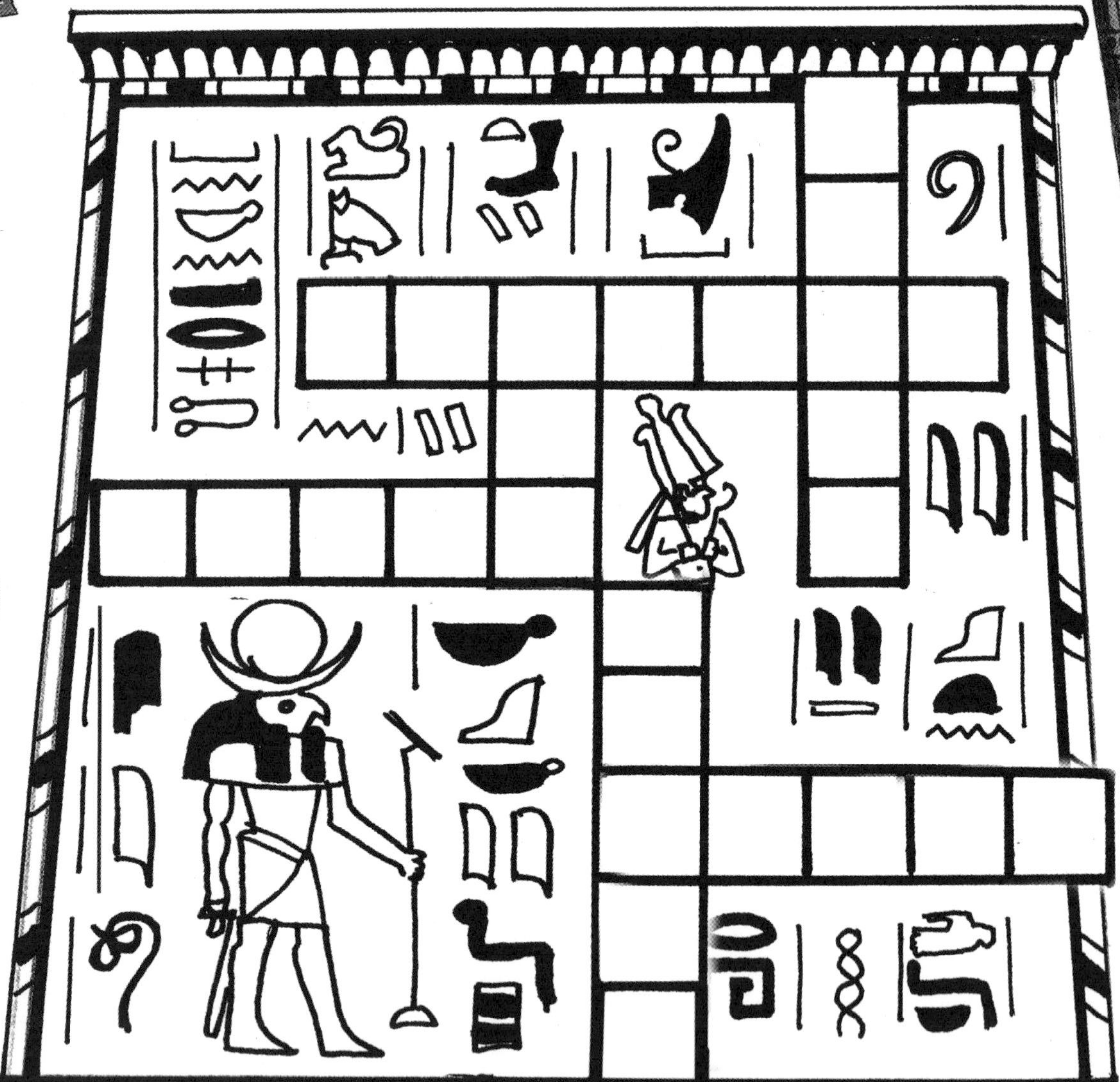

TEMPLE

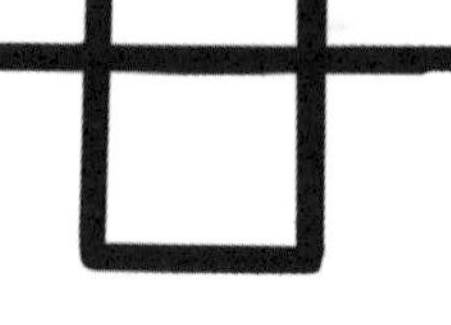

SWORD

CHARIOT

Wordsearch 2

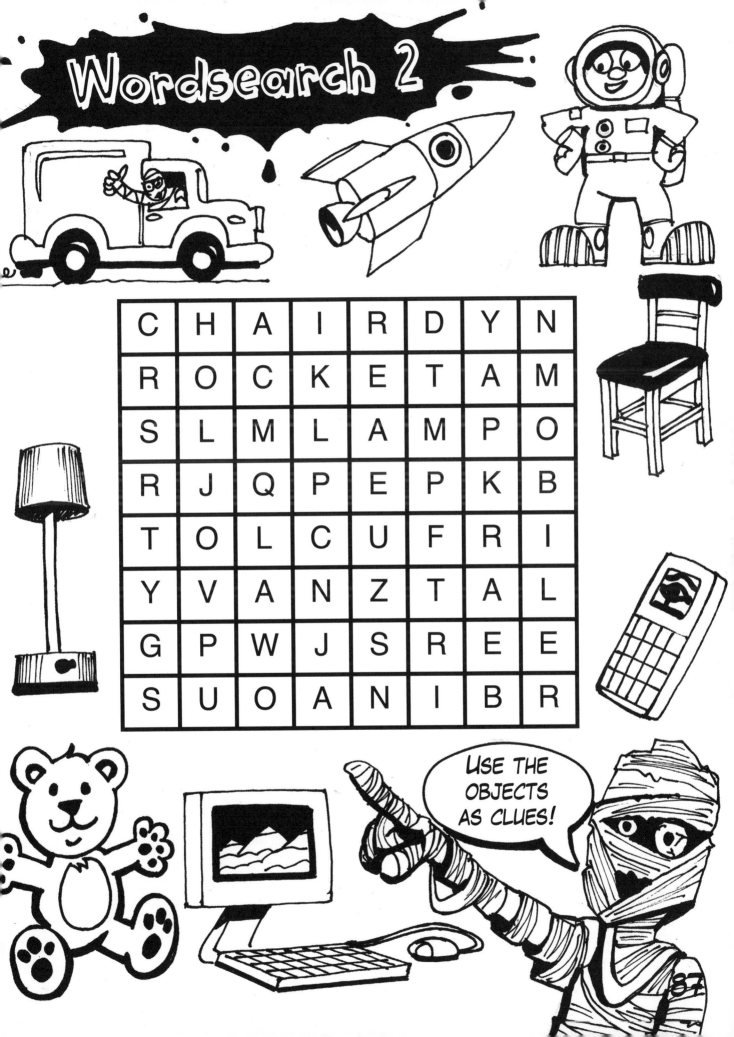

C	H	A	I	R	D	Y	N
R	O	C	K	E	T	A	M
S	L	M	L	A	M	P	O
R	J	Q	P	E	P	K	B
T	O	L	C	U	F	R	I
Y	V	A	N	Z	T	A	L
G	P	W	J	S	R	E	E
S	U	O	A	N	I	B	R

USE THE OBJECTS AS CLUES!

Mix up humans and animals!

Splat-a-fact

QUEEN HENUTTAWY'S MUMMY WORE A WIG MADE OF BLACK STRING. SHE HAD SO MUCH STUFFING IN HER CHEEKS THAT HER FACE EXPLODED!

Where in the world?

Which part of the world do these mummies come from?

A

GREENLAND MUMMIES

B

THIS ANDEAN MUMMY WAS PROTECTED BY A CAIRN OF STONES.

C

THE FRANKLIN EXPEDITION EXPLORERS DIED IN 1845.

D

SOME SOUTH AMERICAN PEOPLES PRESERVED THE HEADS OF ENEMIES.

E

ANICENT INCAS ARE BELIEVED TO HAVE SACRIFICED CHILDREN

USE THE LETTERS AND NUMBERS TO MATCH UP EACH OF THE MUMMIES WITH WHERE THEY WERE FOUND IN THE WORLD.

F
JEREMY BENTHAM DIED IN 1832 AND HIS HEAD AND SKELETON ARE PRESERVED IN A UNIVERSITY.

G

THIS MUMMY WAS PRESERVED BY SMOKING IT OVER A FIRE.

H

6
7
8
9
10

OTZI THE ICEMAN WAS SO WELL PRESERVED THAT PEOPLE THOUGHT HE WAS A RECENT MURDER VICTIM.

I

11

K

FOOD, COSMETICS AND SILK WERE PLACED NEXT TO THIS MUMMIFIED BODY.

J

THIS IRON AGE MAN WAS HANGED OR STRANGLED TO DEATH AND THROWN INTO A PEAT BOG.

THIS BODY WAS PLACED IN AN UNDERGROUND PASSAGE CALLED A 'CATACOMB.'

91

ANSWERS

P4 - HIEROGLYPHS

K I N G   T U T

P5 - LEAD HORUS TO THE MASTABA

P8 - MATCH THE MAGIC BRICKS

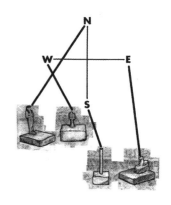

P9 - MATCH THE ORGAN TO THE JAR

P14/15 - SPOT THE DIFFERENCE

P16 - MUMMY SUDOKU 1

1	2	3	4
3	1	4	2
2	4	1	3
4	3	2	1

P17 - MUMMY MAZE

P18/19 - MATCH THE ARTIFACTS TO THE BOXES

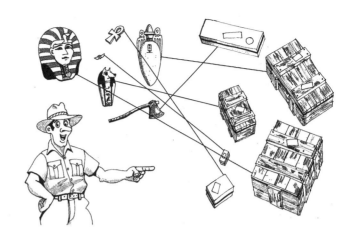

P20/21 - HOW MANY SCARAB BEETLES IN THE TOMB?

ANSWER: 6

P34/35 - HOW MANY MUMMIES CAN YOU FIND?

ANSWER: 40

P27 - JOIN THE DOTS

P44/45 - FIND THE MUMMY CASES

P48/49 - LINK THE ANIMALS WITH THEIR MUMMIES

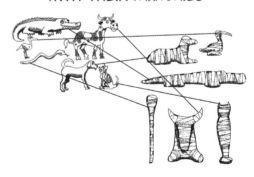

P50/51 - HOW MANY MUMMIES IN THE TOWN?

ANSWER: 18

P54 - WORDSEARCH 1

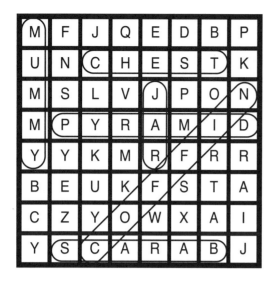

P55 - MUMMY CROSSWORD 1

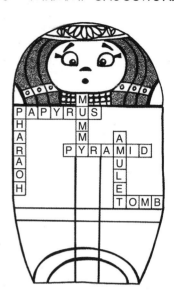

P58/59 - MATCH THE EGYPTIANS TO THE SILHOUETTES

P60/61 - FIND THE SARCOPHAGUS (THERE ARE SIX SCARAB BEETLES)

P64 - HELP THE ARCHAEOLOGIST FIND THE MUMMY!

P67 - MUMMY SUDOKU 2

4	2	1	3
3	1	2	4
1	3	4	2
2	4	3	1

P72/73 - MATCH MUMMY AND SARCOPHAGUS

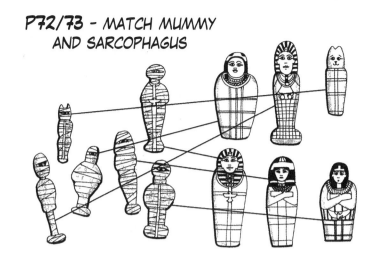

P77 - FIND THE TOMB GOODS (THERE ARE TWELVE IN TOTAL)

P78/79 - I'M A MUMMY, GET ME OUT OF HERE!

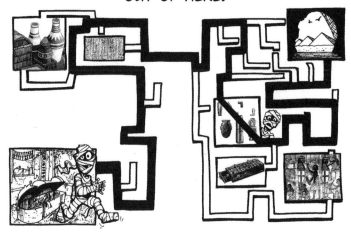

P83 - FIND THE TOMB ENTRANCE

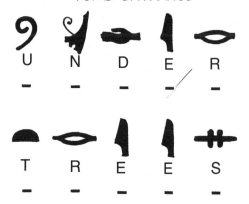

U N D E R

T R E E S

P86 - MUMMY CROSSWORD 2

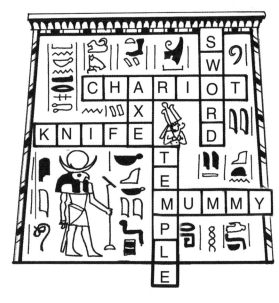

P87 - WORDSEARCH 2

P90/91 - WHERE IN THE WORLD?

1=C
2=D
3=B
4=E
5=A
6=F
7=K
8=H
9=J
10=I
11=G